Percy the Small Engine

THE REV. W. AWDRY

WITH ILLUSTRATIONS BY
C. REGINALD DALBY

RANDOM HOUSE ☖ NEW YORK

Britt Allcroft's Thomas & Friends based on The Railway Series by The Rev W Awdry
Copyright © Britt Allcroft (Thomas) LLC 1999
All rights reserved under International and Pan-American Copyright Conventions.
Published in the United States by Random House, Inc., New York, and simultaneously
in Canada by Random House of Canada Limited, Toronto.
Originally published in Great Britain in 1956 as Book 11 in The Railway Series.
First published in this edition in Great Britain in 1999 by Egmont Children's Books Limited.
THOMAS & FRIENDS is a trademark of Britt Allcroft Inc in the USA, Mexico and Canada
and of Britt Allcroft (Thomas) Limited in the rest of the world.
THE BRITT ALLCROFT COMPANY is a trademark of The Britt Allcroft Company plc.
Library of Congress Catalog Card Number: 00-105263
ISBN 0-375-81224-5
Printed in Italy   March 2001   10 9 8 7 6 5 4 3 2
www.randomhouse.com/kids
www.thomasthetankengine.com
RANDOM HOUSE and colophon are registered trademarks of Random House, Inc.

**DEAR CHRISTOPHER, AND GILES, AND PETER,
AND CLIVE,**

Thank you for writing to ask for a book about Percy.
He is still cheeky, and we were afraid (Sir Topham Hatt
and I) that if he had a book to himself, it might make him
cheekier than ever, and that would never do!

But Percy has been such a Really Useful Engine that
we both think he deserves a book. Here it is.

THE AUTHOR

Percy and the Signal

P ercy is a little green tank engine who works in the Yard at the Big Station. He is a funny little engine and loves playing jokes. These jokes sometimes get him into trouble.

"Peep peep!" he whistled one morning. "Hurry up, Gordon! The train's ready."

Gordon thought he was late and came puffing out.

"Ha ha!" laughed Percy, and showed him a train of

dirty coal cars.

Gordon didn't go back to the Shed.

He stayed on a siding thinking how to get Percy back.

"Stay in the Shed today," squeaked Percy to James.
"Sir Topham Hatt will come and see you."

James was a conceited engine. "Ah!" he thought.
"Sir Topham Hatt knows I'm a fine engine, ready for

anything. He wants me to pull a special train."

So James stayed where he was,
and nothing his Driver and
Fireman could do would
make him move.

But Sir Topham Hatt
never came, and the other
engines grumbled
dreadfully.

They had to do James' work as
well as their own.

At last an Inspector came. "Shake a wheel, James," he said crossly. "You can't stay here all day."

"Sir Topham Hatt told me to stay here," answered James sulkily. "He sent a message this morning."

"He did not," retorted the Inspector. "How could he? He's away for a week."

"Oh!" said James. "Oh!" And he came quickly out of the Shed. "Where's Percy?" Percy had wisely disappeared!

When Sir Topham Hatt came back, he *did* see James, and Percy too. Both engines wished he hadn't!

James and Gordon wanted to get Percy back, but Percy kept out of their way. One morning, however, he was so excited that he forgot to be careful.

"I say, you engines," he bubbled, "I'm taking some freight cars to Thomas' Junction. Sir Topham Hatt chose me specially. He must know I'm a Really Useful Engine."

"More likely he wants you out of the way," grunted James.

But Gordon gave James a wink. . . . Like this.

"Ah yes," said James, "just so. . . . You were saying,
Gordon . . . ?"

"James and I were just speaking about signals at the junction. We can't be too careful about signals. But then, I needn't say that to a Really Useful Engine like you, Percy."

Percy felt flattered.

"Of course not," he said.

"We had spoken of 'backing signals,'" put in James. "They need extra special care, you know. Would you like me to explain?"

"No, thank you, James," said Percy airily. "I know all about signals." And he bustled off importantly.

James and Gordon solemnly exchanged winks!

Percy was a little worried as he set out.

"I wonder what 'backing signals' are?" he thought.

 "Never mind, I'll manage. I know all about signals." He puffed crossly to his freight cars and felt better.

He saw a signal just outside the station. "Bother!" he said. "It's at 'danger.'"

"Oh! Oh! Oh!" screamed the freight cars as they bumped into each other.

Presently the signal moved to show "line clear." Its arm moved up instead of down. Percy had never seen that sort of signal before. He was surprised.

" 'Down' means 'go,' " he thought, "and 'up' means 'stop,' so 'upper still' must mean 'go back.' I know! It's one of those 'backing signals.' How clever of me to find that out."

"Come on, Percy," said his Driver, "off we go."

But Percy wouldn't go forward, and his Driver had to let him "back" in order to start at all.

"I am clever," thought Percy. "Even my Driver doesn't know about 'backing signals.' " And he started so suddenly that the freight cars screamed again.

"Whoa! Percy," called his Driver. "Stop! You're going the wrong way."

"But it's a 'backing signal,'" Percy protested, and told him about Gordon and James. The Driver laughed and explained about signals that point up.

"Oh dear!" said Percy. "Let's start quickly before they come and see us."

But he was too late.
Gordon swept by with the
Express and saw everything.
The big engines talked
about signals that night.
They thought the subject
was funny. They laughed a
lot. Percy thought they were
being very silly!

Duck Takes Charge

"D o you know what?" asked Percy.

"What?" grunted Gordon.

"Do you know what?"

"Silly," said Gordon crossly, "of course I don't know what, if you don't tell me what what is."

"Sir Topham Hatt says that the work in the Yard is too heavy for me. He's getting a bigger engine to help me."

"Rubbish!" put in James. "Any engine could do it," he went on grandly. "If you worked more and chattered less, this Yard would be a sweeter, a better, and a happier place."

Percy went off to fetch some coaches.

"That stupid old signal," he thought. "No one listens to me now. They think I'm a silly little engine and order me about.

"I'll show them! I'll show them!" he puffed as he ran about the Yard. But he didn't know how.

Things went wrong, the coaches and freight cars behaved badly, and by the end of the afternoon he felt tired and unhappy.

He brought some coaches to the station and stood panting at the end of the platform.

"Hello, Percy!" said Sir Topham Hatt. "You look tired."

"Yes, sir. I am, sir; I don't know if I'm standing on my dome or my wheels."

"You look the right way up to me," laughed Sir Topham Hatt. "Cheer up! The new engine is bigger than you and can probably do the work alone. Would you like to help build my new harbor at Thomas' Junction? Thomas and Toby will help, but I need an engine there all the time."

"Oh yes, sir. Thank you, sir!" said Percy happily.

The new engine arrived the next morning. "What is your name?" asked Sir Topham Hatt kindly. "Montague, sir; but I'm usually called 'Duck.' They say I waddle; I don't really, sir, but I like 'Duck' better than Montague."

"Good!" said Sir Topham Hatt.
" 'Duck' it shall be. Here,
Percy, come and show
'Duck' around."

The two engines went
off together. At first the
freight cars played tricks,
but they soon found that
playing tricks on Duck was a
mistake! The coaches behaved well,
though James, Gordon, and Henry did not.

They watched Duck quietly doing his work. "He seems a simple sort of engine," they whispered. "We'll have some fun."

"Quaa-aa-aak! Quaa-aa-aak!" they wheezed as they passed him.

Percy was cross, but Duck took no notice. "They'll get tired of it soon," he said.

Presently the three engines began to order Duck about.

Duck stopped. "Do they tell you to do things, Percy?" he asked.

"Yes, they do," answered Percy sadly.

"Right," said Duck, "we'll soon stop *that* nonsense." He whispered something. . . . "We'll do it tonight."

Sir Topham Hatt had had a good day. There had been no grumbling passengers, all the trains had run on time, and Duck had worked well in the Yard.

Sir Topham Hatt was looking forward to hot buttered toast for tea at home.

He had just left the office when he heard an extraordinary noise. "Bother!" he said, and hurried to the Yard.

Henry, Gordon, and James were *wheeeeeshing* and snorting furiously, while Duck and Percy calmly sat on the switches outside the Shed, refusing to let the engines in.

"STOP THAT NOISE!" he bellowed.

"Now, Gordon."

"They won't let us in," hissed the big engine crossly.

"Duck, explain this behavior."

"Beg pardon, sir, but I'm a Great Western Engine. We Great Western Engines do our work without fuss, but we are *not* ordered about by other engines. You, sir, are our Controller. We will of course move if you order us, but begging your pardon, sir, Percy and I would be glad if you would inform these — er — engines that we only take orders from you."

The three big engines hissed angrily.

"SILENCE!" snapped Sir Topham Hatt. "Percy and Duck, I am pleased with your work today, but *not* with your behavior tonight. You have caused a disturbance."

Gordon, Henry, and James snickered.

They stopped suddenly when Sir Topham Hatt turned on them. "As for you," he thundered, "you've been worse. You made the disturbance. Duck is quite right. This is my railway, and I give the orders."

When Percy went away, Duck was left to manage alone.

He did so . . . easily!

Percy and Harold

P ercy worked hard at the harbor. Toby helped,
but sometimes the loads of stone were too heavy,

and Percy had to fetch them for himself. Then he would push the freight cars along the wharf to where the workmen needed the stone for their building.

An airfield was close by, and Percy heard the airplanes zooming overhead all day. The noisiest of all was a helicopter, which hovered, buzzing like an angry bee.

"Stupid thing!" said Percy. "Why can't it go and buzz somewhere else?"

One day Percy stopped near the airfield. The
helicopter was standing quite close.

"Hello!" said Percy. "Who are you?"

"I'm Harold. Who are you?"

"I'm Percy. What whirly great arms
you've got."

"They're nice arms," said Harold,
offended. "I can hover like a bird.
Don't you wish *you* could hover?"

"Certainly not; I like my rails,
thank you."

"I think railways are slow," said Harold in a bored
voice. "They're not much use and quite out of date." He
whirled his arms and buzzed away.

Percy found Toby arranging freight cars.

"I say, Toby," he burst out, "that Harold, that stuck-up whirlybird thing, says I'm slow and out of date. Just let him wait, I'll show him!"

He collected his freight cars and started off, still fuming.

Soon above the clatter of the freight cars, they heard a familiar buzzing.

"Percy," whispered his Driver, "there's Harold. He's not far ahead. Let's race him."

"Yes, let's," said Percy excitedly, and quickly gathering speed, he shot off down the line.

The Guard's wife had given him a thermos of tea. He had just poured out a cup when the van lurched, and he spilled it down his uniform. He wiped up the mess with his handkerchief and staggered to the front platform.

Percy was pounding along, and the freight cars screamed and swayed while the van rolled and pitched like a ship at sea.

"Well, I'll be ding-dong-danged!" said the Guard.

Then he saw Harold buzzing alongside and understood.

"Go on, Percy!" he yelled. "You're gaining."

Percy had never
been allowed to run
fast before; he was
having the time of
his life!

"Hurry! Hurry!
Hurry!" he panted to
the freight cars.

"We-don't-want-to; we-don't-want-to," they
grumbled, but it was no use. Percy was bucketing along
with flying wheels, and Harold was high and alongside.

The Fireman shoveled for dear life, while the Driver was so excited he could hardly keep still.

"Well done, Percy," he shouted, "we're gaining! We're going ahead! Oh good boy, good boy!"

Far ahead, a "distant" signal warned them that the wharf was near. Shut off steam, whistle, "Peep, peep, peep, brakes, Guard, please." Using Percy's brakes too, the Driver carefully checked the train's headlong speed.

They rolled under the Main
Line and halted smoothly
on the wharf.

"Oh dear!" groaned Percy.
"I'm sure we've lost."

The Fireman scrambled to the cab
roof. "We've won! We've won!" he
shouted, and nearly fell off in his
excitement.

"Harold's still hovering. He's looking
for a place to land!"

"Listen, boys!" the Fireman called. "Here's a song for Percy."

Said Harold helicopter to our Percy, "You are slow!

"Your Railway is out of date and not much use, you know."

But Percy, with his stone cars, did the trip in record time;

And we beat that helicopter on Our Old Branch Line.

The Driver and Guard soon caught
the tune, and so did the workmen on
the wharf.

Percy loved it. "Oh thank
you!" he said. He liked
the last line best of all.

Percy's Promise

A mob of excited children poured out of Annie and Clarabel one morning and raced down to the beach.

"They're the Vicar's Sunday School," explained Thomas. "I'm busy this evening, but the Stationmaster says I can ask you to take them home."

"Of course I will," promised Percy.

The children had a lovely day. But at teatime it got very hot. Dark clouds loomed overhead. Then came lightning, thunder, and rain. The children only just managed to reach shelter before the deluge began.

Annie and Clarabel stood at the
platform. The children scrambled in.

"Can we go home, please,
Stationmaster?" asked the Vicar.

The Stationmaster called Percy. "Take the children
home quickly, please," he ordered.

The rain streamed down on Percy's boiler. "Ugh!"
He shivered and thought of his nice dry shed. Then
he remembered.

"A promise is a promise," he told himself, "so
here goes."

His Driver was anxious. The river was rising fast. It foamed and swirled fiercely, threatening to flood the country any minute.

The rain beat in Percy's face. "I wish I could see,
I wish I could see," he complained.

They came down a hill and found themselves in water. "Oooh my wheels!" shivered Percy. "It's cold!" But he struggled on.

"Oooooooooooooooshshshshshsh!" he hissed. "It's sloshing my fire."

They stopped and backed up the coaches and waited while the Guard found a telephone.

He returned, looking gloomy.

"We couldn't go back if we wanted," he said. "The bridge near the junction is down."

The Fireman went to the Guard's van carrying a hatchet.

"Hello!" said the Guard. "You look fierce."

"I want some dry wood for Percy's fire, please."

They broke up some boxes, but that did not satisfy the Fireman. "I'll need some of your floorboards," he said.

"What! My nice floor," grumbled the Guard. "I only swept it this morning." But he found a hatchet and helped.

Soon they had plenty of wood stored in Percy's bunker. His fire burned well now. He felt warm and comfortable again.

"Buzzzzzzzzzzzzzzzz! Buzzzzzzzzzzzzzzzz! Buzzzzzzzzzzzzzzzz!"

"Oh dear!" thought Percy sadly. "Harold's come to laugh at me."

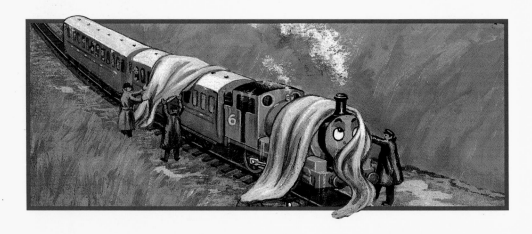

Bump! Something thudded on Percy's boiler. "Ow!" he exclaimed in a muffled voice, "that's really too bad! He needn't *throw* things."

His driver unwound a parachute from Percy's indignant front.

"Harold isn't throwing things at you," he laughed, "he's dropping hot drinks for us."

They all had a drink of cocoa and felt better.

Percy had steam up now. "Peep peep! Thank you, Harold!" he whistled. "Come on, let's go."

The water lapped
his wheels. "Ugh!"
he shivered. It crept up
and up and up. It reached
his ash pan, then it sloshed
at his fire.

"Oooooooooooooooshshshshshshshshshshshsh!"

Percy was losing steam, but he plunged bravely on.
"I promised," he panted, "I promised."

They piled his fire high with wood and managed to
keep him steaming.

"I *must* do it," he gasped, "I must, I must, I must."

He made a last great effort and stood, exhausted but triumphant, on rails that were clear of the flood.

He rested to get steam back, then brought the
train home.

"Three cheers for Percy!" called the Vicar, and the
children nearly raised the roof!

Sir Topham Hatt arrived in Harold. First he thanked the men. "Harold told me you were — er — great, Percy. He says he can beat you at some things . . ." Percy snorted. ". . . but *not* at being a submarine." He chuckled. "I don't know what you've both been playing at, and I won't ask! But I do know that you're a Really Useful Engine."

"Oh sir!" whispered Percy happily.

OTHER TITLES IN
THE RAILWAY SERIES